J. and W. Grimm

LITTLE RED RIDING HOOD

Text by Sabrina Saponaro

Illustrations by Baraldi

Translated by Jean Grasso Fitzpatrick

BARRON'S

Woodbury, New York/London/Toronto/Sydney

Once upon a time, there was a little girl who was loved by everyone who knew her. And because she always wore a little cape and hood made of red cloth, everyone called her Little Red Riding Hood.

Little Red Riding Hood lived with her mother in a pleasant town quite near a great forest. Her house was white, with a red roof. It sat in a meadow beside a stream sparkling with cool, clear water. When animals came to drink at the stream, Little Red Riding Hood loved to skip about and play with them. Yes, she was a happy, care-free girl—only sometimes was she just a little bit naughty.

Now Little Red Riding Hood had a grandmother whom she loved dearly. This grandmother was a nice old woman with snow-white hair who lived on the other side of the forest in a small house filled with flowers.

When Little Red Riding Hood went to her grandmother's house, she usually walked along the big road that passed through town. There was another, shorter path that cut right through the forest, but it was only safe when the woodsmen were there chopping wood. The wild animals of the forest were afraid of the men. Whenever they heard chopping, they stayed in their dens, far from the path.

One day Little Red Riding Hood's mother made some doughnuts. She called her daughter and said, "Grandmother is sick. Go see her and take these goodies to make her feel better."

"I'll go right away," answered Little Red Riding Hood. "If I take the path through the forest, I'll get there sooner. Besides, I'll be able to pick flowers for Grandmother."

Her wise mother added, "You would be better off following the main road. But if you really want to get there faster, you may go through the forest. Just don't stop to talk with anyone. And never step off the path—not even to pick the flowers!"

Little Red Riding Hood promised to obey her mother. Then she combed her hair and put on her cape and hood. She filled the basket with doughnuts, put the handle over her arm, and skipped off into the forest.

It was a calm, clear day. The birds chirped and hopped from branch to branch. In the grass, the flowers glistened with dewdrops. Mushrooms grew on the moss under the big trees.

Little Red Riding Hood was walking happily along the path, when all of a sudden a big, hungry wolf sprang out from behind a bush.

The wolf wanted to gobble up the tasty-looking little girl right away, but he knew he couldn't. He could hear the woodsmen chopping all around them. Besides, if he grabbed Little Red Riding Hood here, the little birds would send out an alarm, and the woodsmen would come running with their sharp axes.

So the wolf came up to the little girl and pretended to be kind. "Where are you going, my pretty little thing?" he asked.

Little Red Riding Hood didn't know what a wicked creature the wolf was. And she wasn't at all afraid of him. She even forgot her mother's advice not to talk to anyone she met. Instead, she smiled and answered, "I'm going to see my grandmother, who is sick. I'm bringing her these goodies."

"Where does your grandmother live?" asked the wolf.

"At the edge of the forest, past the mill, in the little house all by itself just before the village," replied Little Red Riding Hood.

The wolf walked along the path with the little girl for a little while. Then he said, "Look at all these beautiful flowers! Why don't you stop and pick some for your grandmother? I wish I could help you, but I must be on my way. Good-bye and good luck." And he disappeared into the forest.

Little Red Riding Hood thought about what the wolf had said. She looked around and saw the rays of the sun dancing through the tree branches. There were so many flowers in the meadow! She thought, "It's still early. I will pick a bouquet for Grandmother. That will make her very happy!"

Soon the churchbells rang out from the nearby town. That meant it was getting late. But Little Red Riding Hood didn't notice. She just kept picking flowers and chasing butterflies.

Meanwhile the wolf was hurrying through the woods. He took a shortcut, arrived at Grandmother's house, and knocked at the door, "Rat-tat-tat!"

"Who is it?" called the grandmother.

"I am your granddaughter," whispered the wolf, imitating the little girl's voice. He added, "I am bringing you a basket of goodies from Mother."

The grandmother, who was in bed, said, "I am too weak to open the door for you. Just pull the latch, and it will open."

The wolf did as he was told, and as soon as he was in the door, he jumped on the poor grandmother and ate her all up in one bite. Then he licked his chops, put on the old woman's clothes and cap, slipped under the covers, and waited.

Soon Little Red Riding Hood arrived and knocked on the door, "Rat-tat-tat!"

"Who is it?" mumbled a hoarse voice.

"I am Little Red Riding Hood," she called out. "But what a strange voice you have, Grandmother!"

"I have a bad cold," answered the wolf. "I am too weak to let you in. Just pull the latch, and the door will open."

So Little Red Riding Hood went inside and walked toward the bed. Only the old woman's cap could be clearly seen. The wolf had managed to hide most of his hairy body under the covers.

The little girl was surprised at how strange her grandmother looked. "Oh, grandmother, what long arms you have!" she exclaimed.

"The better to hug you with, my dear!"

"Oh, grandmother, what long ears you have!"

"The better to hear you with, my dear!"

"Oh, grandmother, what big red eyes you have!"

"The better to see you with, my dear!"

"Oh, grandmother, what big teeth you have!"

"The better to eat you with!" growled the wolf. And he leaped out of bed and ate the little girl up in one bite.

When his stomach was full, the wolf went back to bed and fell sound asleep.

Just then a hunter passed by. He stopped by the window to say hello, as he did every day, but he was surprised to hear snoring. "I'd better take a look," he thought. "Something is wrong!"

He went inside and walked toward the bed. Instead of the poor old woman, there was the wolf, fast asleep.

"You wicked beast," the hunter shouted. "I've got you now!"

And he pulled out his knife and killed the wolf. Then out of the wolf's belly jumped Little Red Riding Hood. "How dark it was in there!" she said. "How frightened I was!"

Next came her grandmother, just barely alive. The old woman felt much better, however, when she had eaten some of the delicious doughnuts in Little Red Riding Hood's basket.

And Little Red Riding Hood thought, "As long as I live, I'll never disobey my mother again!"

Everyone was happy and safe. And before they went to sleep that night, the birds of the forest sang a song of joy.